DO NOT REMOVE
CARDS FROM POCKET

THE TEDDY BEAR TREE

BARBARA DILLON

THE TEDDY BEAR TREE

ILLUSTRATED BY DAVID ROSE

William Morrow and Company
New York 1982

Copyright © 1982 by Barbara Dillon

All rights reserved. No part of this book may be reproduced or utilized in any form or by any means, electronic or mechanical, including photocopying, recording or by any information storage and retrieval system, without permission in writing from the Publisher. Inquiries should be addressed to William Morrow and Company, Inc., 105 Madison Ave., New York, N.Y. 10016.

Printed in the United States of America.
1 2 3 4 5 6 7 8 9 10

Library of Congress Cataloging in Publication Data

Dillon, Barbara.
  The teddy bear tree.
  Summary: From the buried glass eye of an ancient teddy bought at a rummage sale grows a strange tree that bears surprising fruit.
  [1. Teddy bears — Fiction. 2. Fantasy] I. Rose, David S., 1947- ill.
II. Title.
PZ7.D57916Te [Fic] 82-2301
ISBN 0-688-01447-X   AACR2
ISBN 0-688-01450-X (lib. bdg.)

CONTENTS

To my friend Elaine

1

THE MYSTERY BEAR

"I sure hope I find a good bear at the rummage sale," Bertine Lewis said to her mother on a sunny Saturday morning in spring.

"There are usually quite a few stuffed animals on the toy table," Mrs. Lewis said, as she herded Bertine and her older sister, Lucy, into the car. "But we need to get to the church early, before everything's been picked over."

"You had a nice little bear last summer, but you left him on the beach," Lucy said, climbing into the back seat.

"Don't remind me," groaned Bertine, settling herself next to Lucy. "I get really sad every time I think of poor Willis sitting inside that sand castle all alone."

"But you've still got Howard," said Lucy. "He's not a bad bear."

"Howard's sort of a clunk, though." Bertine sighed and absently checked a scab on her right knee. "Besides, he's too big to take places. I think he's happiest just sitting quietly by himself."

"Well, I'm hoping to find some nice dessert

dishes," said Mrs. Lewis, backing the car out of the garage. "Bertine, don't stick your hand out the window."

"I forgot my money!" cried Lucy, when they were halfway down the driveway.

"She's going to make us late, and all the animals will be gone," Bertine fumed.

Mrs. Lewis stopped the car. "I think I saw your change purse on the kitchen table," she called after Lucy, as she ran back to the house.

"Hurry!" Bertine cried. "Before all the bears get bought."

Ten minutes later the Lewises pulled into the church parking lot.

"Watch out for cars," Mrs. Lewis warned, as Bertine and Lucy jumped out of the back seat.

There were already a number of people browsing among the long wooden tables set out on the church lawn. Piled on top of the tables were books and trays of costume jewelry and handbags and electric toasters and frying pans and glass pitchers and sets of dishes and ashtrays and coffeepots and butter dishes and bedspreads and flowerpots and breadbaskets and even a few old portable radios and TV sets.

"I'll meet you in twenty minutes in front of the food booth," Mrs. Lewis called after the girls, who were hurrying off in opposite directions. "Hold on to your change purse, Lucy."

Bertine threaded her way across the wide church lawn, eagerly quickening her step as she approached the toy table. At one end, in a big, untidy mound, she saw an assortment of dolls. There were girls in grimy dresses and rumpled wigs smiling bravely, rubbery babies, some quite naked, and stuffed animals in various shapes and sizes.

"I need a bear like anything," Bertine muttered, picking up a long-necked giraffe. Beneath him lay a slightly soiled white fur cat, next to whom rested an enormous pink elephant and a floppy-eared gray rabbit. Under the rabbit curled a green plush snake wearing a bow tie.

"No bears!" cried Bertine, digging urgently to the bottom of the pile. Without much hope, she raised a corner of the plastic cloth that covered the table, on the slim chance that a few items had been stored below. Sure enough, next to a pile of blocks was a

doll's rocking chair. Sitting in it, comfortably shaded from the sun, was a small, mud-colored bear. Bertine squatted down to examine him more closely. He was very old. There were worn patches in his fur, and his head looked as though it needed to be sewed on more securely. He was not at all the kind of bear she had in mind.

"Isn't he cute?" said the lady standing behind the toy table. "I was just about to make room for him up top. He's our mystery bear. This morning he suddenly appeared in with all the other toys. But no one remembers who donated him, and none of us has laid eyes on him before today. It's just as if he arrived at the rummage sale all by himself."

"How much does he cost?" Bertine asked warily.

"Twenty-five cents," the lady told her. Bertine had a dollar in change in her jeans pocket. She looked hard at the bear. Then she bent down and lifted him from his chair. His dark, shiny eyes, she decided, were his best feature, and one of them was hanging by a thread.

"Your mom could easily sew that back in," the toy lady assured her.

He was certainly not much of a bear. Still, he only cost a quarter, and Bertine never could resist a bargain. Carefully she counted out a dime and three nickels.

"Enjoy your bear now," the toy lady said cheerily, peeling the price tag from the sole of his foot. But already Bertine was regretting her purchase. Despite his nice eyes, he really was a pretty dingy-looking teddy. Spending twenty-five cents on him had been a mistake.

Bertine worked her way slowly to the baked-goods table, trying to hide the bear behind her in case she ran into any of her friends. Standing in front of the coffee cakes was her mother.

"I was lucky," Mrs. Lewis said, holding out a brown paper bag to Bertine. "Look at these darling dessert dishes. Just the kind I was looking for." Then her eye fell on Bertine's bear.

"He's cute, Bert," she said brightly. But somehow

Bertine got the feeling her mother was just being polite.

"Look what I got," said Lucy, hurrying up a second later with a gaily colored game box tucked under one arm. "Chutes and Ladders. And there're no pieces missing either." She glanced at Lucy's bear. "Yuk, what's that gross thing?"

"Mom, Lucy's being mean," said Bertine, scowling at her sister.

"No, she isn't," said Mrs. Lewis, who was always quick to head off an argument. "Here, girls, help me pick out some cupcakes for dinner."

As soon as the Lewises arrived home, Lucy ran to show her game to her father, who was raking up twigs and dead leaves in the yard.

"And I picked up these sweet dessert dishes," Mrs. Lewis said, holding up one for Mr. Lewis's inspection. "They'll go beautifully with my pink place mats."

"Very nice," said Mr. Lewis, leaning on his rake. "What did you get, Bert?"

"Oh, just this," said Bertine, reluctantly holding out her bear.

14

Her father looked at it and smiled. "That's a bear that's gotten a lot of wear."

"He's a mystery bear," Bertine told him earnestly. "The lady at the toy table said so."

"The only mystery about him," said Lucy in a taunting voice, "is how he got so dirty."

"Get lost, Lucy," cried Bertine, and she flounced angrily into the house, slamming the screen door behind her.

Shortly after lunch, Bertine's best friend, Betsy Bissell, who lived across the street, stopped by to show Bertine what she had bought at the sale.

"Look," she said, proudly displaying a black velvet evening purse with a rose embroidered on the clasp. "And it only cost ten cents."

Bertine looked at the purse enviously. She wished she had seen it before Betsy had.

"What did you get, Bert?" Betsy asked. Bertine was tempted to lie and tell her nothing, but Betsy discovered the bear sitting behind a floor lamp on the porch. She picked him up and examined him carefully all over. "He smells funny, Bert," was all she had to say.

"He's a mystery bear, though," Bertine said. "He arrived at the rummage sale all by himself. The saleslady said so."

Betsy looked thoughtfully at the bear. She looked at her velvet purse. "Mystery or not," she said, "I'd rather have my bag."

So would I, thought Bertine. But, of course, she wasn't going to tell Betsy that.

Just before dinner, Bertine came into the kitchen with her bear. From the window, she could see Lucy on her hands and knees at the end of the garden.

"What's she doing?" Bertine asked her mother. Mrs. Lewis glanced up from the pot of tomato sauce she was stirring on top of the stove.

"Planting zinnia seeds," she said.

"I want to plant some too," said Bertine. She rushed out the kitchen door, holding her bear by one arm.

"Can I help?" she asked, kneeling down beside her sister.

"If you don't make a mess of it," Lucy said bossily, shaking some seeds out of a paper packet. Carefully

Bertine took a seed and dropped it into one of the little holes Lucy had dug with her trowel.

"Now you pat dirt over the top of the hole like this," Lucy said, showing her how.

Poppy, a young Labrador retriever who lived two blocks away, came bounding across the backyard to see what the girls were doing. Poppy was the neighborhood thief. She had been known to steal mittens and caps and balls and bones and once even a pair of men's underpants wrestled from somebody's clothesline. Now her eyes lit up as she spied Bertine's bear lying on the ground. Immediately she galloped over and picked him up in her mouth. Bertine looked up from her planting and saw Poppy shaking the bear back and forth like a mop.

"Poppy, bad dog!" she cried, jumping to her feet.

"Bad Poppy, drop it," commanded Lucy, making a lunge at the dog.

But Poppy, thinking Lucy wanted to play, turned and streaked off across the lawn, almost colliding with Mr. Lewis, who was coming up the driveway, after fertilizing the azalea bushes down at the mailbox.

"What in the world's the matter?" he asked, looking first at Bertine, who had covered her face with her hands and was weeping noisily into them, and then over his shoulder at Lucy, who was sprinting after the delighted Poppy.

"Poppy stole my new bear," wailed Bertine.

"That dog!" said Mrs. Lewis, coming out from the kitchen to see what all the commotion was about. "Nothing's safe when she's around."

"Now I have no more little bear," Bertine sobbed, peeking out between her fingers to see if perhaps her mother or father looked sorry enough to buy her a new, decent one.

"Poppy's run off into the woods with Bertine's bear," panted Lucy, coming back up the driveway. "I'm not going after her into all that poison ivy." She looked critically at her sister. "I don't know why Bertine's making such a fuss. She didn't like her bear that much anyway."

"Well, but it was a bad way to lose the old fellow," said Mr. Lewis, putting his arm around Bertine. "Stolen by a thief in the night."

"Let's go in and eat," said Mrs. Lewis. "We're

having your favorite, Bertine — spaghetti."

Lucy suddenly bent down and picked something up from the grass. "Look what I found," she said. In the palm of her hand was a small, shiny, dark thing — the mystery bear's eye.

"It looks like one of your seeds, Lucy," said her father. Lucy handed the eye to Bertine. "Maybe you want to keep it," she said. "As a remembrance."

"Come inside, everybody," Mrs. Lewis urged, "before the spaghetti gets cold."

All through dinner Bertine kept fingering the sad little eye in her jeans pocket. It was all that was left of the unlucky mystery bear. Perhaps she should bury it, she thought, and put a marker over the spot, like a gravestone.

As soon as dinner was over and she had helped carry the dishes to the kitchen, Bertine ran upstairs and pulled open her desk drawer. Under an overdue library book, she found what she was looking for — an old popsicle stick.

She got out her crayons and with the black one wrote *Bear* along its length. In a spot at the end of the garden, a short way from Lucy's zinnia seeds, she buried the eye and stuck the stick in the ground above it. Not much of a grave, she reflected, but better than nothing.

2

THE MYSTERY TREE

The next morning, bright and early, the girls ran outside to see if Lucy's seeds had started to come up. They hadn't, but right by Bertine's popsicle stick was a big green shoot.

"Just a weed," Lucy said disdainfully, when Bertine pointed it out to her.

"How come it wasn't there last night?" Bertine demanded.

"It probably was, and you just didn't notice," Lucy said through a yawn.

But Bertine was certain she would have noticed. "I don't think this thing is a weed," she said to herself. "It may not be a regular plant, but it's no weed either. I'm sure it isn't."

The next day she was even more certain; the shoot had grown almost a foot high. On the following day, branches, lots of them, were sprouting in all directions from the main stem. By midweek, buds had appeared.

"What kind of crazy tree can it be anyway?" Mr. Lewis said, scratching his head in perplexity as he gazed at the slender branches bending beneath the weight of their swollen buds.

"Sometimes in science class we see movies of trees

and plants that burst into bloom before your very eyes, just the way this one is doing," said Lucy.

"But that's a camera trick," said her mother. "Our tree is for real, and the way it's behaving is a little scary. I mean, when is it ever going to stop growing?"

"It really is the darnedest thing," agreed Mr. Miller from next door. He had come over with all his plant books to see if he could find a picture in any of them like the Lewises' tree. "The leaves resemble those of the sassafras," he noted. "But they're much bigger. The bark looks like a hickory and the buds. . . ." He gave a helpless shrug. "What can I tell you? I've never seen anything like it before."

"That's because you've never seen a tree that grew from a teddy-bear's eye, Mr. Miller," Bertine told him. "Maybe I'm the first person ever to have planted one."

Mr. Miller smiled and patted Bertine's head. "One thing I *am* sure of, young lady: Your mysterious tree has not grown from a glass eye."

That was exactly what her mother and father said too. But Bertine didn't care. She knew that the mystery bear's eye was growing into something wonder-ful. So did the other children on the street.

"Can I have one of the buds when it blossoms?" asked Betsy Bissell on Friday afternoon.

"I want one too," said her younger brother, Jus-tin, who tagged after Betsy wherever she went.

"I think I should have a flower," said Drew Nichols from across the street. "My mom loves flowers, and I could give it to her for her birthday."

"Maybe we could have a backyard party when the buds open," suggested Lucy. "We could call it a Grand Opening," she added cleverly.

"I hope the tree blooms before I go to visit my grandmother," said Kathy Ritchie, who had pedaled up from the corner with her sister Joyce.

"Maybe the tree will keep on growing till it's so big it knocks your house down," said Joyce in a hopeful voice. "The buds are already about the size of grapefruits."

"If the tree has real, honest-to-goodness flowers on it, I would like one," said Mr. Miller's daughter, Peachy. "I collect all kinds of flowers and press them flat in a book."

"I'm not giving all my blossoms away before they even bloom," said Bertine, who had no intention of sharing what was growing on her tree with anyone, not even Betsy Bissell.

Each day before she left for school, Bertine ran outside to see how much the tree had grown during the night.

"Look," said Lucy one morning, "that big bud there on the lower branch looks as if it had a nose." She gave a disdainful sniff. "Trust Bertine to grow a bud with a nose."

But Bertine, overjoyed with her gardening success, merely smiled and turned to admire another bud that in the past eight hours had developed two interesting bulges that might or might not be a pair of ears.

The Lewises awoke Saturday morning to a hard, driving rain; Bertine spent most of the day indoors looking out the window at her tree.

"Should I put the beach umbrella over it?" she asked her mother anxiously.

"Honey, the rain is good for growing things," Mrs. Lewis told her.

26

"But the buds are so heavy," Bertine worried. "If they get much soggier, they'll be lying right on the ground."

Toward evening, the rain became less steady and finally stopped altogether. Bertine put on her rubbers and went out into the dripping garden with a hand towel to blot the buds dry. Their knobby shapes beneath her fingers felt as mysterious as the packages in a grab bag. Briskly she drew down a branch directly above her head, sending a shower of raindrops into her hair. As she pressed her towel against the bud on the end of it, a tiny muffled voice cried out "Careful!"

Bertine sprang back in alarm. "That can't have come from the tree," she whispered. "There's no such thing as a talking tree."

Cautiously she tilted the bud again. But except for the squawking of a lone blue jay sitting atop Mrs. Lewis's bird feeder, there was complete silence in the backyard. Bertine tried tipping a few other buds. Some of them gave thin little cries, as dolls do when you turn them over on their stomachs. Some were soundless.

"Weird," muttered Bertine, shaking her head. "Just about the weirdest thing I've ever known." She had all she could do to keep from peeling back the tightly furled green sheaths enclosing the buds; her fingers particularly itched to unveil the bud that she thought had spoken.

"No," she told herself sternly. "I will let them all open by themselves. I don't want to hurt whatever's inside." She stared longingly at the wet tree. "But I can hardly wait to see what's going to come pop' ping out."

3

THE BLOOMING

Bertine awoke Sunday morning as the sky was beginning to turn rosy. The moon, pale and wafer thin, still lingered in the west as though it wanted to stay around for a while to see what the day might bring. Shivering a little in the cool air, Bertine slipped into her bathrobe and ran barefoot down the stairs.

Quietly she let herself out the kitchen door and hurried through the dew-drenched grass to the garden.

There in the clear morning light stood her tree, its
dark-green mitten-shaped leaves looking scrubbed
and bright after the rain. Every one of its mysterious,
intriguing, bulging buds had opened wide at last to
the new day. Overnight, each of them had flowered
into a beautiful, perfectly formed teddy bear!

"Oh, wow!" said Bertine, too overcome to do
anything but stand and stare. Unlike the blooms of
an ordinary flowering tree, the bear blossoms were
different colors. Two were the warm yellow of a
maple leaf in fall; two white ones, one large and one
small, had coats snowy as apple blossoms. One stout
bear was pearly gray; another was the deep russet of
a horse chestnut. Hanging side by side on the same
branch were twins, chubby oatmeal-colored bears
with fat stomachs. Just below them was a thin coal
black bear with a felt tongue protruding saucily from
his mouth.

"They are all so beautiful," breathed Bertine,
stretching out her hand to the black bear. His fur
was slightly moist to the touch and gave off a rather

30

pleasant odor of damp plush and newly turned earth. Timidly, fearing she might hurt him, Bertine plucked the black bear from the tree. The little green stem by which he was attached to his branch snapped crisply, like a fresh string bean. Still scarcely able to believe her wonderful tree was real, she picked the yellow bears, both of whom dropped easily into her outstretched hands. The gray and russet bears, swinging from the same branch by their paws, seemed a bit reluctant to let go; Bertine had to tug a little. Next she took hold of a sturdy brown bear clinging to a branch above her head. This one was a nice size, she thought, neither too large nor too small, and she liked the rich molasses color of his coat.

"He makes either number six or number seven," she muttered, wresting him gently from the tree to which he was fastened by his left ear.

"I'm number six," the bear said in a clear voice, as he plopped into her arms. "I believe there are ten of us altogether."

Bertine gave a squeal of delight. "You're the one who told me to be careful yesterday, aren't you?" she asked him. The bear made no response. Bertine gave him a little shake and turned him over on his back to see if there was a cord to pull to make him talk again. Though he remained silent, the teasing sparkle in his eye convinced her he could say anything he wished. She also got the feeling that this bear had a mind of his own.

Giving him a hasty hug, she added him to her growing pile of bears. I've got to find something to put them in, she decided, and hurried into the garage in search of her wheelbarrow. Lowering the bears

 into it, she trundled them back out to the tree. Next, panting with excitement, she picked off the white bears and had only just freed the oatmeal-colored twins when her mother appeared on the lawn in her housecoat.

"I don't believe this," gasped Mrs. Lewis, when she saw the bears in the wheelbarrow. She cupped her hands to her mouth and called up to Mr. Lewis, who was still in bed. "Come down here, Doug! We

have something wonderful to show you!"

Mr. Lewis, looking tousled and sleepy, stuck his head out of an upstairs window.

"What's Bertine got there?" he asked. "Without my glasses it looks like a load of stuffed bears in that barrow."

"It is!" shouted Lucy, peering out her window. "The teddy bear tree has bloomed!"

"I've got ten of them!" Bertine cried, flushed with triumph as she laid the last three in the wheelbarrow. She could hardly wait to get the bears to some quiet spot where she could look them over and sort them out and welcome each one personally.

"What's going on here?" asked Mr. Miller, peering over the top of his rhododendron bush. He had stepped out to get his newspaper and heard the commotion in the Lewises' backyard.

"Bertine's tree has given birth to a big batch of bears," cried Lucy with a giggle.

"Ray, can you believe this?" said Mr. Lewis, who had come out on the lawn in his bathrobe. "The darned thing's actually blossomed into stuffed bears!"

"No, I don't believe that," said Mr. Miller, joining

the Lewises and the bears. "Not for a minute." He looked at the wheelbarrow full of teddies, and then he looked suspiciously from one Lewis to another.

"How many·of you actually saw the bears grow‑ing on the tree?" he demanded.

"Well, really only Bertine," began Mrs. Lewis. "But—"

"I thought so," said Mr. Miller with satisfaction. "It's amazing what an eight‑year‑old thinks she sees sometimes. Why, you should hear the wild things our little Peachy tell us."

"There were bears growing on every single branch," Bertine told Mr. Miller with dignity. "I don't make things up."

But Mr. Miller had turned his attention from Ber‑tine to her tree. He moved a step closer and looked carefully at the lower limbs.

"Is it just my imagination, or is it beginning to wilt?" he asked. Everybody turned to stare at the teddy bear tree. Sure enough, its branches were droop‑ing like a weeping willow's. Leaves were shriv‑eling and turning brown, and many of them were already floating gently to the ground.

"I suppose you're going to tell me that the crop of bears was too much for it," Mr. Miller said with a smile of amusement.

"I think maybe it was," said Lucy regretfully. "I was hoping that we'd have bears all summer long."

"A new batch every week or so would have been fun," agreed Mrs. Lewis.

Mr. Miller threw up his hands. "Batty," he muttered to himself. "Every last one of them. The next thing you know they'll be telling me the bears can walk and talk. I'm going home to read my paper."

A few minutes later Peachy Miller, wild with excitement, came running into the Lewises' backyard. Bertine's tree had, by this time, folded up like an umbrella and was listing so badly that most of its naked branches were touching the ground. But on the screened porch sat Bertine, proud as a queen, her lap piled high with the fruit of the withered tree.

"Oh, what terrific bears!" exclaimed Peachy. She sat down on the couch next to Bertine and tried to pick up the black bear, but Bertine covered him possessively with her hand.

At that moment, Drew Nichols came hurrying

into view, followed by Betsy Bissell and her brother, Justin. "Some bunch of bears," said Drew, ignoring Bertine's frown as he stepped on the porch without invitation. "I don't think even the Nature Center has a tree like yours, Bertine."

"Bertine, could I hold the little white one?" asked Justin, barely catching the screen door before it closed on his fingers.

"No, you'll get it dirty," Bertine told him.

"His hands are clean, honest," said Betsy. "He really loves bears, Bertine."

"So do we," called Kathy Ritchie, suddenly appearing from behind the big clump of rhododendrons at the side of the porch. Her sister, Joyce, was trotting at her heels.

"Bertine won't let anyone touch them, though," said Justin, eyeing the white bear longingly.

"I know, let's take the bears for a ride in my wagon," suggested Kathy Ritchie.

But Bertine shook her head. "The bears want to rest," she said. "They're tired."

"I'm not," whispered a voice. Bertine didn't have to guess which of the bears on her lap had spoken.

"Did you say something, Bertine?" Kathy asked.

"No," said Bertine quickly. "But I was just thinking that maybe I'd better take the bears into the house now."

"We could have a picnic in our backyard," Kathy persisted. "And make funny paper hats for them."

"They don't like parties," said Bertine, casually placing her hand over Number Six's mouth. "And they especially hate hats."

"How do you know?" asked Peachy Miller.

"I just know," Bertine answered.

"You're really being piggy, Bertine," said Betsy severely.

"She sure is," agreed Joyce Ritchie. "She wouldn't even let Justin hold the little one."

"They're mine, all of them," declared Bertine. And she didn't care in the least that her neighbors called her selfish or that every one of them went home in a huff. After all, she had ten beautiful bears. Who could ask for anything more?

After her friends' departure, Bertine carried the bears up to her room, all except the russet-haired one, which her mother insisted she give to Lucy.

"I don't see why Lucy should get one," grumbled

Bertine. "She didn't think that much of my first little bear when I bought him at the fair. She even said he was gross."

"Yeah, but who found his eye in the backyard?" Lucy reminded her.

"Yeah, but who thought to plant it?" Bertine retorted.

"For heaven's sake, Bert, I bet you have more teddies than any girl in town," said Mrs. Lewis in exasperation. "I do think Lucy is entitled to at least one of them."

"Anyway, you have so much junk in your room, I don't know where you'll find space for even nine bears," said Lucy, triumphantly raising her new bear to her shoulder. She looked thoughtfully at her sister. "If you gave me one more of them, Bert, then you'd have eight, one for each year of your life. Wouldn't that be nice?"

"You're not getting another bear, Lucy, so forget it," Bertine said. "Besides, next February when I'm nine, I'd be short a bear."

Lucy shrugged and moved off toward her room, hugging her teddy. "I'm going to call him Noel," she said. "Noel Lewis is a good name."

Noel *was* a good name, Bertine reflected as she arranged the remaining bears around her room; she was sorry she hadn't thought of it herself for the talking bear, who at that moment tumbled from her bed onto the floor. Bertine stared in amazement as he scrambled to his feet and stood looking slowly around the room.

"Oh, this is really nice, Bertine," he said, glancing with approval at her new desk, the exercise bar that her father had put up in her doorway the week before, the poster of lion cubs hanging over the bookcase. Then he padded quickly across the floor to where the big bear, Howard, sat stiffly on a little wooden bench. Gently the talking bear reached out a paw and touched Howard on the nose.

"Tch, tch, what a shame," he murmured, shaking his head.

"What's wrong?" Bertine asked. She was sitting cross-legged on the floor, utterly fascinated with the bear's inspection of her room.

"I'm afraid your friend is not quite right," he whispered, tapping his head meaningfully. "Can't you tell by the glassy look in his eye? Maybe he was

not given enough stuffing or perhaps the wrong kind was used. We must be very kind to him always, Bertine." The bear's glance shifted to the doll's bed in the corner.

"Who's that in the cage?" he asked suspiciously.

"That's my doll Emily," Bertine explained. "And that's not a cage; it's a bed."

"Does she bite?" the bear asked. "I notice she's got little teeth."

"Oh, I'm sure Emily wouldn't bite," Bertine hastened to assure him.

"What's on top of your desk?" he asked next. "Lift me up so I can see." Bertine picked him up and put him on the desk, where he examined with interest her jar of colored pencils and the eraser shaped like a cat. "What color is this?" he asked, pointing to the green pencil.

"Green," Bertine told him. "And this one is red and that's blue."

Stepping to the edge of the desk, the bear raised one paw to his forehead, shading his eyes like an explorer standing on a mountain peak.

"Who are those piddly little people over there?" he asked, pointing toward her bureau.

"Those are my foreign dolls," Bertine explained. "One is from Mexico, one's from Holland, one's —"

"Never mind," he said with a wave of his paw. "They're too small to amount to much." Then he sat down, dangling his chocolate-colored legs over the edge of the desk. "Think of a good name for me, Bertine," he commanded. "I don't know many names yet, so I'll leave it up to you."

"Let's see," said Bertine, wrinkling her brow. "How about Tizzy?"

"I hate it," said the bear.

"Wink?" Bertine suggested.

"Might do for one of the others, but not for me."

"Larry?"

The bear pondered. "Try again," he urged.

"Jerry?" Bertine asked hopefully.

"Not bad," said the bear. "But not that good either."

Bertine had a sudden inspiration. "How about Joel?" she suggested. "Rhymes with Noel, which is the name of Lucy's bear."

"Joel," the bear repeated. "Yes, that's a fine name. I like it very much. I will be Joel. Good thinking, Bertine. Now how about names for the others?"

"I'll work on it," Bertine promised. "But don't rush me. Names aren't that easy to come up with." She sat down in the desk chair and lifted Joel onto her lap. "Now it's my turn to ask a few questions," she told him.

But Joel wasn't listening. "I want to see what's under your bed," he said, struggling to get free. "It looks as if you've got a lot of interesting stuff under there."

"It's just junk," Bertine said. "Sit still and listen to me. I want to know about the mystery bear. Who was he and how come a tree grew from his eye when I planted it in the garden?"

"Mystery bear?" repeated Joel in a puzzled voice. "I don't know anything about any mystery bear. The first thing I remember was finding myself curled up in a cozy little green cocoon. I didn't know the

cocoon was really a bud, of course. I didn't even
know what green was till you showed me the pencils
on your desk. Anyway, I was content just to doze
and dream inside my little nest, but after a while I
began wanting to stretch my arms and legs, and
suddenly one morning my bud split open, and I
found myself hanging by my ear from a tree in a
garden with a lot of other bears. Isn't it lucky it was
your garden we grew in?" Joel asked, leaning his
head contentedly against Bertine's stomach.

"But why is it you can walk and talk and the
others can't?" Bertine persisted.

"I expect I was just born a gifted bear," said Joel
simply.

"I expect you were," agreed Bertine. "But I love
the others too, you know, even though they're
nonwalkers and talkers."

"Oh, they can walk and talk," Joel assured her.
"But not when human beings are around. They've
already told me how glad they are to be here and
how they're looking forward to having fun with
you — every single day."

Bertine looked around at her new big family, at

the nine pairs of eyes staring at her expectantly. And for the first time she felt a twinge of uneasiness. Entertaining all those bears was going to be a big job. But the uneasiness passed just as quickly as it had come. "We'll have a wonderful time," she promised Joel. "All of us, all summer long."

4

BEAR TROUBLE

That afternoon Bertine went with her father to the Wayside Nursery to buy plants for the garden.

"Do you want to come too, Luce?" Mr. Lewis asked, as he got into the car.

"Nope, I'm taking Noel over to Margaret Garvey's," Lucy said. "I don't mind sharing my bear, which is more than some people are willing to do." She glanced significantly at Bertine, who was already sitting in the back seat with Joel on her knee and the other bears lined up on the seat next to her.

"Lucy's just jealous, because I have nine bears and she has only one," she whispered to Joel. "And she'd be even more jealous if she knew you could talk."

"Well, don't expect me to say anything to her," Joel whispered back. "I'm a one-child bear, Bertine. I talk only to you."

"Still, I'd love to see Lucy's face if you suddenly said to her, 'Lucy, Bertine turns much better cart-wheels than you, even if you are two years older.'"

"What's a cartwheel?" Joel asked.

"Bert, if I didn't know you were alone back there, I'd swear you were having a conversation with someone." Mr. Lewis laughed and glanced at Bertine in the rearview mirror.

"I'm making up a story, Dad," Bertine said quickly. "For English class."

Bertine very considerately tried taking all the bears out of the car at the nursery. Joel, the two white bears, and the gray one got to see the flats of pansies and the rosebushes. The two yellow bears were shown the geraniums and the hanging baskets. But before the oatmeal twins and the black bear had a chance to look over the snapdragons and zinnia seedlings, Mr. Lewis had finished making his purchases and announced he was going.

"Don't worry," Bertine assured the black bear, giving his paw a squeeze. "I'll make it up to you later." Nevertheless, Bertine was given hard looks all the way home by those whom she had not had a chance to take around.

That night after she had brushed her teeth and put on her pajamas, Bertine climbed into bed with her nine bears. Sleeping with such a crowd was not easy; she kept rolling over on arms and legs and paws and snouts. By morning, everyone but Joel had fallen on the floor. He lay peacefully at her side, gazing up at the ceiling.

Bertine brought all the bears downstairs with her to breakfast. Mr. Lewis had to scoop some from his chair so he could sit to drink his coffee. And when he moved two to the kitchen counter, one fell into the sink and had to be patted dry with paper towels.

"There's no room for me in here," Lucy complained a little while later, when she went into the den to finish up her homework before school. "There're bears in all the chairs."

"Bears also on the stairs," Mrs. Lewis noted, when she carried the clean laundry up to the linen closet.

"Layers of bears," said Mr. Lewis that evening, as he moved seven or eight from the hall table where they were sitting on top of the morning's mail.

"That's the way it should be," said Bertine serenely. "The more bears the better."

The next day after school Bertine decided to go over to Betsy Bissell's. Carrying Joel and the black bear and the twins, she ran across the street and around to the Bissells' side porch where Betsy and Kathy were sitting side by side with coloring books and crayons.

"Hi," Bertine called out cheerfully.

"Hi," said Betsy in a rather distant voice.

Kathy, without even looking up from her book, whispered loudly, "Why doesn't Bertine go back home and take her boring bears with her?"

Bertine could hardly believe her ears. Her cheeks burning with indignation, she turned and stalked off across the lawn, hoping that Joel didn't notice how close she was to tears.

"Well, if Betsy Bissell wants to play with that stupid Kathy Ritchie, let her," she said to the bears in a choked voice. "We have plenty of interesting things to do at home. We can go shopping with Mom. We can have a tea party with Emily and the others. We can even ask Lucy to play Parcheesi. So the heck with Betsy and Kathy." She glanced at Joel, waiting for him to say something, but he was wearing one of his No Comment expressions.

Bertine sighed as she crossed the street to her own house. All the same, if the girls had asked her to stay and color, she would have gladly. The bears could have sat and watched.

"Bertine, if you don't come this minute, I'm going to go without you," Mrs. Lewis called crossly half an hour later. She was sitting in the car waiting for Bertine to come out of the house.

Bertine was trying to decide which bears to take

along to the grocery store. The decision was hard, because they all looked as though they wanted to go. Her mother honked again, and Bertine snatched up Joel and rushed downstairs, leaving the others staring reproachfully after her.

At dinner that night, all the bears were brought to the dining room to watch the family eat. They sat on the extra chairs and on the windowsill and on the floor. The small white bear perched on the dining-room table suddenly keeled over into the creamed corn. The black one, propped up on the sideboard, somersaulted into Mr. Lewis's path as he walked past to the kitchen and narrowly avoided being stepped on. And Joel, sharing a chair with Bertine, suddenly gave a loud hiccup.

"I knew you had too many potato chips this afternoon," Mrs. Lewis said, frowning at Bertine. "I think it might be a good idea if you skipped the butterscotch pudding."

Before Bertine could protest, Lucy asked if she could swap Noel for the big white bear. Bertine said absolutely not, and the meal ended in a huge argument.

"Why were you all so naughty at dinner?" Bertine asked Joel peevishly, as they climbed into bed that night.

"We didn't mean to be," Joel told her. "But we're young and excitable and haven't learned table manners yet. We need a lot of taking care of — all of us." He turned his head on the pillow to stare at Bertine. "This brings me to a very important point. Can you stay awake while I discuss it with you?"

"Sure," said Bertine, raising herself on one elbow. "Shoot."

"It's about the others," he told her. "We must find homes for them, Noel not included, of course."

Dumbfounded, Bertine stared at Joel. "But the other bears already have a home. You know that. They live here with us."

"There are too many of them," Joel explained. "You can't possibly give each one the attention a teddy really needs. Besides, you must have noticed how unhappy your friends all looked the other day because you were the one with all the bears. Didn't that make you sad?"

What Bertine had noticed was that her friends

had envied her. And that didn't make her sad in the least. In fact, she found that being envied was quite a nice feeling.

"So what we will do," continued Joel briskly, "is to give each of your friends a bear. I will stay here naturally, but the others need to have someone to play with."

Bertine looked at Joel indignantly. "I'm not giving away any of them," she told him. "I like bears. I love having them. I'm keeping the whole bunch."

"You're selfish, Bertine," said Joel. "You haven't learned to share."

"No way will I share a bear," Bertine said stubbornly.

"That is your final word?" Joel asked.

"Absolutely," said Bertine.

"We'll see," said Joel. "Good night."

His eyes didn't close, of course, but Bertine had the feeling that he either fell asleep with them open or had suddenly gone deaf, because he wouldn't speak another word to her, even though she tried to engage him in an argument. Even a pinch on the bottom brought no response. At length, she gave up trying to get him to talk and with a sigh settled back in bed. Sleepily she drew Joel up against her. He had a soft but sturdy body and fit very nicely just under her chin.

"Strange little Joel, strange little bear," she murmured. She gave a big yawn and the next minute had fallen sound asleep.

When Bertine opened her eyes next morning, the first thing she noticed was that there were two bears missing from the room — one of the twins and the black bear. But before she had a chance to question Joel, her father appeared in the doorway in his pajamas looking very cross.

"Bertine, what's been going on up here?" he demanded.

Bertine sat up in bed. "What are you talking about, Dad?" she asked, startled.

"I'm talking about the mess in the bathroom. I suppose you'll tell me that bear sitting on top of the john did it."

Bertine glanced at Joel, who lay on his back, smiling pleasantly at the ceiling. Hastily she hopped out of bed and hurried down the hall to see the damage

for herself. There sitting innocently on the toilet lid was the twin, wearing a beard of shaving cream and looking like a Santa Claus. Shaving cream was sprayed all over the bathroom mirror, in the tub, the sink, and around the counter. There were even globs of it on the windowsill.

"I don't know how this happened," Bertine declared. "Maybe Lucy did it. I saw her trying to shave her legs the other day."

"Well, whoever is responsible is going to be in a lot of trouble if they touch any of my stuff again," Mr. Lewis warned grimly.

He was in for an even greater shock, however, when, twenty minutes later, he discovered his brief-case lying open on the floor of the downstairs hall. Papers were scattered everywhere, and in the midst of them sat the black bear, straight as a poker, staring into space.

"I'm going to miss my train. I'm going to be late for my meeting," Mr. Lewis cried, giving the black bear a rude shove as he dropped to his knees to gather up the contents of the briefcase.

Bertine stood watching her father, too scared even to offer to help him pick up his papers.

"What do you know about this?" she whispered to Joel, whom she was holding in one arm. But the bear remained silent. If he knew anything, he wasn't telling.

Mr. Lewis had no sooner left the house, grumbling and muttering threats, than Lucy let out a yell from her bedroom. "Look what's happened to Marcella!" she screamed. Down the stairs Lucy flew, holding her favorite doll out in front of her. Someone had rubbed chunks of peanut butter into the doll's curls.

"She's ruined!" wailed Lucy, distractedly lifting one of Marcella's greasy locks between her fingers. She glared at Bertine. "You did this!" she hissed. "I know you did."

"I did not," protested Bertine, backing hastily behind her mother. "Mom, Lucy's going to hit me."

Mrs. Lewis threw up her hands in despair. "What a morning!" she moaned. "And it isn't even eight thirty yet."

"One of the bears put that goop in Marcella's hair, I'm sure of it," Bertine confided, as Mrs. Lewis hurried off to find shampoo for Marcella's hair.

Lucy gave her sister a startled look. "Oh, honestly, Bert," she said. But her voice sounded more anxious than exasperated. "This is really bad," she muttered to herself. "Bertine's freaked out. She's gone bonkers over bears."

That night, however, Lucy's concern for her sister turned to fury. Bertine's marbles had been dumped all over the den, and Lucy stepped on one in her bare feet. Mr. Lewis stepped on a marble too and yelled at Bertine, who tearfully insisted that the bears were the ones who had spilled them. Mr. Lewis then became very stern and commanded Bertine to stop making up silly lies, and Lucy said that she was now certain that Bertine had flipped, to which Bertine replied that she certainly hadn't but that in any event Lucy was a creep, to which Mrs. Lewis responded by ordering both girls to bed at once, even though it was only eight o'clock. All in all, it was not one of the Lewises' better evenings.

Wednesday was half a day at school because of a teachers' meeting, and it was also Mrs. Lewis's bridge-club day — a coincidence that struck her as most unfortunate.

"I want you two to play quietly," she told Lucy and Bertine. "No messes and no naughtiness, understand?" She looked warily from one girl to the other. Ordinarily, her children were trustworthy, but with what had been going on lately, she no longer felt sure of either of them. Only that morning someone had tipped a bottle of nail polish into her cosmetic kit, covering everything with sticky pink enamel.

"I didn't do it," Lucy had said.

"I didn't either," Bertine declared, nervously hiding behind her back the big white bear on whose paw she had caught a glimpse of rosy polish.

"We'll be good, Mom," Bertine quickly promised. She just hoped she could keep an eye on the bears. Monitoring was not easy with so many of them.

"Let's play school," Lucy suggested.

"Okay, but first I'm going to put the bears in my

room," said Bertine. "I'm afraid they'll get into trouble if I leave them lying around."

Lucy, humoring her sister, asked with a mocking smile, "How are you going to make them stay in there? There's no lock on your door."

Bertine looked worried. "Maybe it would be better to have them play school with us. They can be the other pupils. That way I can watch them."

The two girls set up a card table on the porch and carried out books and pads and pencils. Bertine set the bears in rows on the floor.

"You behave now," she told them grimly.

"I'll be the teacher first," said Lucy. "Get out your pencil, Bertine; I'm giving out a math assignment." The bears sat stiffly at attention, staring brightly at the school supplies. From the living room where Mrs. Lewis and her friends were playing bridge, the girls could hear the murmur of voices and an occasional trill of laughter. And then, just as Bertine was about to give Lucy a spelling test, there was a shout from upstairs.

"My Lord, what's happened here?" one of the ladies cried. Bertine glanced in alarm at the bears. She was relieved to see none of them was missing. There was the sound of footsteps hurrying up the stairs, followed by a shriek from Mrs. Lewis.

Together the girls dashed up to their mother's bedroom to see what was going on. They were greeted by an appalling sight. The ladies' purses, which had been left on Mrs. Lewis's bed along with sweaters and jackets, had all been opened and their contents dumped on the floor. Combs and lipsticks and compacts and Kleenexes and laundry slips and marketing lists and appointment cards were scattered everywhere. Tablets and capsules had been shaken out of pillboxes. Wallets lay open, and photos and credit cards were in a terrific jumble. Pennies and nickels and dimes and quarters, not to mention bills, covered the floor as if a money shower had suddenly rained from the ceiling. It was impossible to imagine that the purses ever could be set in order.

"How in the world did this happen?" asked Mrs.

Lewis, looking as if she were about to cry.

Thank goodness it isn't the bears this time, thought Bertine. But all at once her heart sank. Peeking out from under a blue raincoat on the bed was a shiny eye and one reddish brown ear.

"Look!" she croaked to Lucy, pointing to the raincoat.

Lucy recognized the eye and the ear right away. They belonged to Noel, the bear Bertine had given her.

"You should never have left him alone in your room," Bertine whispered disapprovingly.

"But it's crazy, Bert," Lucy mumbled, looking in dismay from Noel to the ladies who were kneeling and sitting on the floor, trying to sort out their belongings. "Teddy bears can't do the kinds of things that have been happening around this house. I know they can't."

"You'd be surprised what they can do," said Bertine, shaking her head. "You'd be absolutely amazed."

"Teddy bears can't do the kinds of things that have been happening around this house. I know they can't," was exactly what Mrs. Lewis said that evening, after she had told Mr. Lewis about the dumping of her friends' purses. Bertine, who happened to be passing the den on her way to the kitchen for a glass of milk, paused to listen.

"And I know it wasn't the girls," Mrs. Lewis continued, "They would never have done such an awful thing."

"No, I don't think they would have either," Mr. Lewis agreed. "So — that leaves only the bears."

"Oh, Doug, it can't possibly be the teddies, can it?" Mrs. Lewis asked nervously.

"Well," said Mr. Lewis with a shrug, "if a person wakes up one morning to find something as nutty as a teddy bear tree in his yard, who's to say that the bears growing on it can't go stumping around getting into trouble?"

"It seems that they can and do," said Mrs. Lewis, sighing, "though I still can hardly believe it."

"We absolutely cannot have a big bunch of badly behaved bears running around here loose," said Mr. Lewis. "That's for sure." There was silence in the den; Bertine waited anxiously to hear what her parents would say next.

"We could insist Bertine keep them caged," Mr.

Lewis suggested. "And if that doesn't work, we may have to come up with some sterner measure."

"Naughty as they are, I could never stand to see them harmed," said Mrs. Lewis.

"No, I wouldn't want that either," agreed Mr. Lewis. "But they must be kept under control. I've about had it with teddy bear high jinks."

At bedtime, Bertine sat Joel on her lap, holding him tightly by both paws.

"Are you the one who is telling the others to do all these terrible things?" she demanded.

"Well, I've given them a few suggestions," said Joel modestly. "But it wasn't my idea to dump your dad's briefcase. Guess who thought that up."

"Who?" Bertine asked gloomily.

"Old Emily," said Joel with a giggle.

Bertine shook her finger at the figure in the doll bed. "Emily, you stay out of this," she warned. She turned back to Joel. "Why are you such bad bears? You're really going to get clobbered, all of you, if you don't shape up."

"We're not bad, Bertine," said Joel earnestly. "We're lovely bears. As for me, I was just trying to

68

help out the others. They need personal attention. They need mothers."

"*I* am their mother," Bertine insisted. "But I can't play with all of them all of the time. They've got to learn about taking turns."

"Not enough time for turn taking," Joel told her. "Pretty soon you'll be grown up and will no longer care about bears. Then we'll all be left sitting forever. We have to make hay while the sun shines. We have to have our good times now." He rested his head persuasively against her arm. "Come on, Bertine. Find us some new homes, what d'ya say?"

"I'll never let you go to a new home, Joel," said Bertine fiercely. "Never."

"Oh, I have no intention of leaving," Joel assured her. "I'm planning to stay on here forever. If you like, we could have one or two others stay too. Three bears would be just the right number."

Bertine sighed and began sucking the end of her pigtail, which was what she always did when faced with a difficult decision. "Well, I'll think about it," she said, as she climbed slowly into bed. "But I'm not making any promises yet, so don't hassle me."

"I wouldn't dream of it," Joel answered meekly.

Bertine lay quietly on her back for a while, watching the reflection of cars' headlights glide smoothly across the far wall of her room. Then she began counting on her fingers and saying names to herself. "If I did decide to find homes for some of the bears," she said at last to Joel, "I think I would keep the little white bear and the black one here with us."

"Hmm," said Joel thoughtfully.

"Why do you say 'hmm' that way?" asked Bertine. "Why don't you say 'Good idea, Bertine'?"

"Because you ought to keep the oatmeal bears," Joel told her. "They are twins, and they shouldn't be separated."

"I like the other two better," said Bertine.

"The white bear would be happier with a baby," Joel declared. "Because of his size and his softness. The black bear, on the other hand, likes a lot of roughstuff. He'd do best with a boy."

"No," said Bertine stubbornly. "The white and the black are staying."

"We'll see," said Joel, and promptly went into one of his nonspeaking trances.

"Boy, what a know-it-all bear," Bertine muttered. "I just might make him sleep on the floor." But she didn't, partly because she feared he would be cold down there and partly because she was beginning to think that even though he was sometimes very bossy, he usually knew what he was talking about.

5

THE TEDDY BEAR BASH

The next morning at breakfast Bertine asked her mother if she could have a party the following day.

"What kind of a party?" Mrs. Lewis asked in surprise. "This is certainly short notice."

"It's a find-a-new-home-for-a-bear party," said Bertine. And when she explained the details to her mother and Lucy, they both thought she had hit on a very good idea.

"I could bake some cookies," Mrs. Lewis said, going to the pantry to see if she had any chocolate chips.

"I'll help too," Lucy volunteered, and that afternoon she and Bertine wrote out invitations to the party. The invitations read:

Come to a Teddy Bear Bash
Lewises' Backyard
Friday, 3:30 PM

"I thought bash meant to hit someone," said Bertine.

"It can also mean a good time," Lucy explained. The girls delivered an invitation to the door of each of Bertine's friends on the street and then hurried back home to work on more party preparations.

Everyone arrived promptly the next afternoon. Mrs. Lewis had set out two pitchers of lemonade and a big platter of cookies on the picnic table. Lucy

74

had found a package of balloons in her desk drawer, and she and Bertine had blown them up and tied them in the branches of the trees. They looked very gay bobbing in the breeze.

"Where are the rest of the bears, Bertine?" asked Peachy Miller, looking at Joel and Noel and the twins sitting together on the picnic bench.

"You'll find out," said Bertine mysteriously. She reached into the pocket of her sundress and drew out a handful of brightly colored cloth strips that she and Lucy had cut from leftover scraps in their mother's sewing drawer. They passed out a strip to each child.

"Hidden around the yard," Bertine told them, "are bears with bows around their necks."

"You have to match up the bows with the strips of cloth in your hand," Lucy explained.

"Let me tell them, Lucy," Bertine said. "It was my idea."

"I helped hide the bears, though," Lucy reminded her.

"Do we get to play with the bears when we find them?" asked Kathy Ritchie.

"You get to keep them," Bertine told her grandly. "Start looking."

With shouts of glee, the children rushed off across the lawn. Bright eyes peered out at them from the secret hiding places Bertine and Lucy had found for the bears.

"Warm, you're getting warm," cried Bertine and Lucy, as a child got close to a bear. Or they called out, "Cold, cold," if he wandered away from one.

Suddenly Betsy Bissell gave a squeal of joy. "I found him, I found my animal!" she exclaimed, as she spied the gray bear, sporting a blue bow around his neck and crouching in back of a rosebush. Bertine thought the bear looked very pleased as Betsy gave him a hug.

"Hey, cool," said Peachy Miller, plucking the big white bear out of a willow tree. "I think I'll call him Wendell, after my uncle."

Justin found his bear, the little white one, huddled under an overturned flowerpot. "Thank you, Bertine," he said, grinning with delight.

"You're welcome, Justin," Bertine answered, giving him a kindly pat on the head.

"Wow, look at mine!" shouted Drew Nichols, grabbing the black bear from in back of a lawn chair. "He looks like a real grizzly, except for the dopey pink bow." Drew snatched off the bear's ribbon and, making loud growling noises, carried him over to the picnic table.

"See, Joyce," said Kathy Ritchie, holding her bear out to her sister. "Our teddy bears are the same color."

"I think they're the best of the whole bunch," whispered Joyce, looking happily from one yellow bear to the other.

Bertine watched with satisfaction as her guests, with their bears, gathered at the table and helped themselves to cookies and lemonade. The pleased

expressions on their faces made her feel very grand and grown up, rather like a fairy godmother. "Have another cookie," she urged everyone. "And help yourself to more lemon-ade. There's plenty."

Lucy was the first one finished. "Let's play some-thing," she said, swatting a bee off Noel's nose.

"How about red rover?" suggested Betsy.

"Giant steps," said Peachy.

"Ring-around-the-rosy," said Justin, knocking over his juice.

"Hide-and-seek," announced Lucy. "I'll even be it."

As the others scrambled to their feet, Betsy leaned over and whispered to Bertine, "Want to sleep over on Friday?"

"Sure," said Bertine eagerly. "And I'll bring my bears."

"I'm going to ask my mom to help us make pajamas for them," Betsy said, giving her own bear an affectionate squeeze. "Wouldn't they look neato in clothes?"

"Yellow would be nice for Joel," Bertine decided. "And the twins could wear pink."

"Green for my guy," said Betsy, jumping up from the picnic bench. As Bertine was about to follow her across the lawn, a gruff little voice at her elbow said, "Blue."

Bertine looked down at Joel, sitting next to the twins. "I like yellow best," she told him.

"Blue," said Joel.

"Yellow," said Bertine.

"Blue," said Joel.

"We'll see," said Bertine, and dashed off around the side of the house in search of a good hiding place.